To: Olivia Rose Kearns – J.S.

Once There Was a
Christmas Tree

A Magical Snow Globe Book
by Jerry Smath

Cartwheel BOOKS

SCHOLASTIC INC.

New York   Toronto   London   Auckland   Sydney   Mexico City   New Delhi   Hong Kong   Buenos Aires

"It's almost Christmas!" said Mrs. Bear. "And we still don't have a Christmas tree!"

"Don't worry," said her husband. "I'll find one."

Mr. Bear took his saw and went deep into the woods.
There he found the biggest tree he could carry
and brought it home.

Mr. Bear put the tree in the living room.
"It's a beautiful Christmas tree,"
said his wife. "But it's much too tall."

"I'll fix that!" said her husband.
With his saw, he cut the tree in half.

Just then Mrs. Bear looked out the window. She saw Mr. Fox pulling his son on a sled. They were going into the woods to look for a tree.

"Why don't we give them the top of our tree?" she said.
Mr. Bear agreed. So Mrs. Bear tied a big bow to the top
of the Christmas tree and took it outside.

"Yoo-hoo! Mr. Fox!" called Mrs. Bear.
"We took our tree and made it two.
One half for us, one half for you."
Mr. Fox was delighted. "Thank you so much," he said. "What
a wonderful present!"

Mr. Fox put the tree on the sled. Then he and his son turned the sled around and pulled it home.

Once the tree was up, the two foxes stood back to admire it.
"It's the prettiest Christmas tree I've ever seen," said the little fox.
His father thought so, too.

They were just about to decorate their tree when Mr. Fox thought of his friend Old Rabbit.

"Old Rabbit lives all alone," he said. "And he doesn't have a tree this year."

"Our tree is big!" said his son. "Why don't we share it with him?"

"Good idea!" said Mr. Fox. So he took his saw and cut their tree in half.

Together Mr. Fox and his son took the top of their Christmas tree to Old Rabbit's house.

When Old Rabbit opened the door, Mr. Fox and his son said,
"We took our tree and made it two.
One half for us, one half for you."

Tears came to Old Rabbit's eyes when he saw their gift. "How kind
of you both," he said.

Old Rabbit brought the Christmas tree into his house and put it in his window.

Next, he put a silver star on top of the tree. Then, one by one, he added the ornaments.

Old Rabbit was almost done when...OOPS! One ornament that looked like a carrot bounced off the tree.

It kept rolling until it stopped by a hole in the floor.

"Thank goodness it didn't fall in!" said Old Rabbit. "That was my favorite one!"

Just as Old Rabbit was about to pick up the ornament, it was
pulled into the hole.

Peeking down into the hole, he saw Mother Mouse and her three children. They were trying to eat the carrot ornament. "Don't eat that!" he shouted. "It's made of wood!"

Old Rabbit saw that the Mouse family was hungry.
So he invited them to dinner.

Afterwards, Old Rabbit and Mother Mouse
chatted and watched the children play.

"It's nice to have friends," said Old Rabbit, smiling.

It was getting late.

Mother Mouse carried her sleepy children home and tucked them into bed.

Old Rabbit went to bed, too, but he could not sleep.
When he looked at his pretty tree in the window, he knew why.
"It's Christmas Eve!" he thought. "The Mouse family should
have a Christmas tree of their own!"

Old Rabbit went to the window and cut the top off his tree.

Quietly he tiptoed over to the hole and slipped the little
tree into the Mouse family's room.

"Merry Christmas," he whispered.
"I took my tree and made it two.
One half for me, one half for you."
Then Old Rabbit tiptoed back to his bed and went to sleep.

Once there was a Christmas tree—

—but sharing made it four.

And Santa Claus left presents under every one.

Library of Congress Cataloging-in-Publication Data available

ISBN: 0-439-72499-6

10 9 8 7 6 5 4 3 2   5 6 7 8 9/0

Printed in China /Fabriqué en Chine /Fabricado en China
First printing, October 2005

Tested for EN71 & ASTM. Liquid is non-toxic. In case of puncture, wash immediately to prevent staining.
Not intended for consumption. Do not ingest. Adult supervision required.

Testé pour EN71 en ASTM. Liquide non toxique. En cas de perforation, laver immédiatement pour éviter les taches.
Non comestible. Ne pas manger. Utiliser sous la surveillance d' un adulte.

Scholastic Ltd, Westfield Road, Southam, CV47 ORA England